A NOTE TO PARENTS

When your children are ready to "step into reading," giving them the right books—and lots of them—is as crucial as giving them the right food to eat. **Step into Reading Books** present exciting stories or information reinforced with lively, colorful illustrations that make learning to read fun, satisfying, and worthwhile. They are priced so that acquiring an entire library of them is affordable. And they are beginning readers with an important difference—they're written on three levels.

Step 1 Books, with their very large type and extremely simple vocabulary, have been created for the very youngest readers. **Step 2 Books** are both longer and slightly more difficult. **Step 3 Books,** written to mid-second-grade reading levels, are for the child who has acquired even greater reading skills.

Text copyright © 1985 by Random House, Inc. Illustrations copyright © 1985 by Marc Brown.
All rights reserved under International and Pan-American Copyright Conventions. Published
in the United States by Random House, Inc., New York, and simultaneously in Canada by
Random House of Canada Limited, Toronto.

Library of Congress Cataloging in Publication Data:
Hautzig, Deborah. Happy birthday, Little Witch. (Step into reading. A Step 2 book) SUMMARY:
Little Witch worries that her birthday party will be a failure unless she can get her friends
to come. 1. Children's stories, American. [1. Witches—Fiction. 2. Parties—Fiction.
3. Birthdays—Fiction]   I. Brown, Marc Tolon, ill.   II. Title.   III. Series.
PZ7.H2888Hap 1985 [E] 85-1796 ISBN: 0-394-87365-3 (trade); 0-394-97365-8 (lib. bdg.)

Manufactured in the United States of America   2 3 4 5 6 7 8 9 0

STEP INTO READING is a trademark of Random House, Inc.

Step into Reading

Happy Birthday, Little Witch

by Deborah Hautzig
illustrated by Marc Brown

A Step 2 Book

Random House 🏠 New York

It was Little Witch's birthday.

All the witches were busy.

They were busy getting ready

for Little Witch's birthday party.

Grouchy Witch was hanging cobwebs.

Cousin Dippy Witch was making
a valentine for Little Witch.
Nasty Witch was making fun
of Dippy Witch.

Mother Witch was baking
a big chocolate frog cake.

Everyone was in a party mood...
everyone but Little Witch.

"This party will be the same
as always," Little Witch told
her bat, Scrubby.

"Aunt Nasty will bust my balloons.
Aunt Grouchy will make it rain.
Why can't I ever have a nice party?"
Then Little Witch had an idea.
"Maybe I can find my friends
Astronaut, Pirate, and Devil!

"When they came trick-or-treating
on Halloween, we had so much fun!
I will ask them to my party,"
she told her cat, Bow-Wow.
"Come on, Scrubby.
Come on, Bow-Wow.
Let's try to find them!"

On her way out Little Witch

stopped in the kitchen.

"Do you need any help, Mother?"

she asked.

Mother Witch stamped her foot.

"When will you stop being so good?"

Mother Witch screeched.

"Just go out!

Get dirty!

And come home late!"

So Little Witch, Scrubby,
and Bow-Wow set off.

"Let's find Astronaut first,"
Little Witch said.
Then she got on her broomstick
and said some magic words:

"Zippity, zappity,
Onion dip,
Fly me to
A rocket ship!"

WHOOSH! She was off!

Bow-Wow shut his eyes

and held on to Little Witch.

Up, up, up they zoomed…
through the clouds,
past the moon,
in between the stars,
and—plunk!—onto a rocket ship.
Little Witch peeked
in the window.

Two astronauts looked out at her.

"Do you see what I see?"

said one surprised astronaut.

"A little witch!" said the other.

"Oh, it's the wrong rocket ship,"
said Little Witch sadly.
"My little astronaut is not here.
Maybe I will have better luck
at finding Pirate."
Then she waved good-bye
to the two big astronauts
and said some more magic words:

"Splishy, splashy,
Bottle of rum,
Pirate ship-py,
Here I come!"

Little Witch flew over the town,

across the sea,

and landed on the deck

of a big black ship.

"Who are you?"
shouted the captain of the ship.
Little Witch said,
"I am just a little witch
looking for my pirate friend."

"You have no friends here,"
growled the captain.
And he made her walk the plank!
But just as Little Witch came
to the end of the plank,
she chanted:

"Jeepers, creepers,
Mouse's ear,
Broomstick, get me
Out of here!"

The broomstick quickly took
Little Witch up, up, and away
from the pirate captain.
"Oh, dear, that was close!"
said Little Witch.
"Now there is only one thing
left to do—
look for Devil."

She said a magic spell:

"Devils are red,
Devils are hot,
I'm coming to find you,
Ready or not!"

Little Witch landed with a bump.

All around her were big pots.

In the pots was something

red and hot.

Something that bubbled and boiled.

Something that smelled good.

"Oh, no!" cried Little Witch.

"It's tomato soup!"

Little Witch had landed

in a tomato soup factory!

"My spells never work right.

I'm just a flop,"

Little Witch said sadly.

Then Little Witch heard someone.

"Hello, little girl,"

said a fat little man.

"Why are you dressed

for Halloween?"

Little Witch said,

"I'm not!

I am a witch.

A real witch.

And today is my birthday.

I am looking for my friends."

The man smiled.

He knew there are no witches.

"Maybe your friends are

in school," he said.

"Hey, maybe they are!"

she said, and then she chanted:

"Hocus-pocus,

Toady stool,

Broomstick, take me

Right to school!"

WHOOSH! She flew off.

And the man was so surprised

that he fell into a pot of soup.

Little Witch landed

outside the school window.

She looked inside.

The teacher was holding something.

"This is Lulu," said the teacher.

"Lulu is Billy's pet mouse."

When Bow-Wow heard "mouse,"

his fur stood up.

Bow-Wow was scared of mice.

He ran away.

"This birthday is the worst.

I cannot find my friends.

And now Bow-Wow is lost."

Little Witch looked for him

in the schoolyard

and down the street.

She even looked in a doghouse.

Finally she gave up.

"Come on, Scrubby, let's go.

Maybe Bow-Wow ran home."

When Little Witch got home,

the house was dark.

She started to cry.

"Scrubby, I think they forgot

about my party."

She opened the door

and then . . .

POP! POP! BANG!

went a room full of balloons.

The lights went on.

And there were all the witches

and Bow-Wow...

and three children.

"Happy birthday, Little Witch!"

everyone cried at once.

A little girl said,

"I'm Milly. I was the astronaut!"

A boy said, "I'm Sam.

I was the pirate."

The other boy said,

"I'm Marcus. I was the devil!"

"We found Bow-Wow," Milly said.

"He was hiding

in a garbage can.

We knew he was your cat.

So we came to bring him back.

Your mother asked us

to stay for your party."

And what a party it was!
Milly, Sam, and Marcus showed
Little Witch how to play
games she never played before!

They played blindman's buff,

pin the tail on the devil,

and musical chairs.

Then Grouchy Witch did make
it rain.
But this time it rained
black and blue jellybeans!

Dippy Witch wished everyone

a happy Fourth of July.

Then she set off

one hundred firecrackers.

"Dippy gets mixed up,"

Little Witch told her friends.

"But we love her anyway."

Everyone ate lots of cake
and lots of candy.
"Candy is so good!"
said Nasty Witch.
"It rots your teeth
so nice and so fast!"

Then Mother Witch gave
Little Witch a present.
It was a big bag of dirt.
"Thank you," said Little Witch.
"Maybe it will help me
not to be so clean."

"No," said Mother Witch.
"It won't. You are just
a good little witch.
You cannot help it.
And the worst part is
I LOVE YOU ANYWAY!"
Mother Witch gave Little Witch
a big birthday hug.

Everyone sang "Happy Birthday."
It was the finest birthday party
Little Witch had ever had.